# When Dad's at Sea

Mindy L. Pelton

Illustrated by Robert Gantt Steele

**Albert Whitman & Company, Morton Grove, Illinois**

To Katherine and Meredith, and to the children and
families of our United States Armed Forces.
—M.L.P.

To my daughter Catherine:
no longer a little girl, but still her Dad's inspiration.
—R.G.S.

Library of Congress Cataloging-in-Publication Data

Pelton, Mindy L.
When Dad's at sea / by Mindy L. Pelton; illustrated by Robert Gantt Steele.
p. cm.
Summary: Emily, whose father is a Navy pilot, has to deal with the
separation of her family while her dad is deployed aboard a ship.
ISBN 0-8075-6339-0 (hardcover)
[1. Military dependents—Fiction.  2. Fathers and daughters—Fiction.  3. Separation (Psychology)—Fiction.]
I. Title: When Dad is at sea. II. Steele, Robert Gantt, ill. III. Title.
PZ7.P3683Wh 2004 [E]—dc22  2003016772

The design is by Carol Gildar.

For information about Albert Whitman & Company,
please visit our web site at www.albertwhitman.com.

Most days, Dad lives with Mom and me in our blue house with an American flag on the porch.

Other days, he lives with pilots, like himself, and sailors on a U.S. Navy ship carrying rows of airplanes.

I miss Dad when he sails to the other side of the world.

All summer long, I knew Dad would have to leave again when school started in the fall. When the time came, he reminded me, "The ship pulls out in three days to go on a cruise."

I felt sad and mad and scared all at once, like a big ball of yarn had gotten tangled inside my stomach. I knew he would be gone for a very long time.

"When are you coming home?" I asked.

Dad said, "I'll be home in six months."

"How many days is that?" I said with a groan.

He thought for a moment; then, his eyes brightened. "I know, I'll show you."

Mom, Dad, and I cut strips of colored paper and shaped one circle for each day Dad would be gone. Then, we linked them all together, forming a long chain. Dad drew hearts on the middle circle to show me the halfway point of his cruise. When we were done, we hung the chain like a streamer on the living room walls.

Dad said, "Take off one circle every night, Emily. I'll come back when the chain is gone."

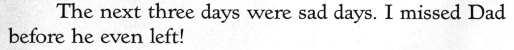

The next three days were sad days. I missed Dad before he even left!

I sat in Mom's chair at mealtimes to be close to him. I watched him pack his clothes into a big metal box with enough toothpaste and shampoo to last forever. Dad winked at me as he folded the pillowcase I painted for Father's Day and stacked it on top of his T-shirts.

I didn't want to fall asleep the night before Dad
had to go. Maybe he wouldn't leave if there were no
more circles left on the chain. I tiptoed through the
darkness into the living room and pulled it off the walls.
It fell with a loud *swish*.

Then I heard the *flap, flap, flap* of Mom's slippers coming toward me from the hallway.

Quickly, I dragged the chain to my room and hid it under the bed.

The next morning, Dad wore his green flight suit to breakfast. The chain was hidden under my bed, but nothing had changed. He was still leaving!

I ran to my room and tore the circles into tiny pieces. When Dad came in, I turned away.

"Emily," he said, "I know you don't understand why I have to go. I don't want to be away from our family, but I have to work in a different place for a while. My job helps keep people safe."

"Don't leave me!" I cried.

Putting his arms around me, Dad said, "When I travel, Mom takes good care of you at home, but I take you with me in my heart."

"Take me in your sea bag!" I begged.

Dad smiled. "I wish I could. When I feel sad because I'm away from the two most special people in the world, I see pictures in my mind. I think of you and Mom waiting for me in our blue house, and I feel better.

"Whenever you miss me you can see pictures, too—just close your eyes and think of me. I'll always be with you."

Dad dried my tears and led me to the living room.
A new chain was hanging on the wall!

"Mom and I made you a new one last night," he
said.

The new chain was better! There were pictures
and words on every circle. The circle in the middle had
colored hearts and candy taped to it.

"I'd better go now," Dad said with a good-bye kiss.
"I'll e-mail you when I get to the ship."

Then he hugged Mom and me and walked to his car. Driving away, he honked and waved just like he always does when he goes on a trip.

I missed Dad all day at school. I wished he had a different job so he could stay home.

That night, Mom said she had a special surprise for story time. She turned on a video.

Dad was on TV! He read my favorite books to me and pretended to talk to my stuffed animals. I laughed when he kissed them good night, like I do. When the video ended, I wanted to watch it again.

Mom said I could take the first circle off the chain once I changed into my pajamas. The circle had a happy face on it and the words, "I love you, Emily."

I curled the paper strip around my fingers until I found a safe place for it. I peeked in the mirror at Dad's picture that Mom had ironed onto the front of my T-shirt. He smiled at me, and I smiled back.

But I cried after Mom tucked me in because Dad wasn't there to kiss me good night. He wouldn't be back until all the circles came down, one day at a time.

I wondered what Dad was doing. I wanted to see pictures in my mind like he does, so I thought about the day our family visited the ship.

I imagined Dad flying off the top deck and over the ocean. I saw him catch the wire with the tail hook of his plane as he came in for a landing. When I was too tired to see any more pictures, I hugged my T-shirt and fell asleep.

Mom checked the computer every day to see if
we had an e-mail from Dad. Most days we did. I liked
getting photos. My favorite was the one of him standing
by his bunk bed holding a picture he drew for me.
It was a stick man with his arms wide open, saying,
"I love you this much!"

On Halloween, Dad surprised us by calling from
the ship. He told Mom and me about three special food
days for all of the sailors—Meatball Mondays, Taco
Tuesdays, and Fish Fridays.

It sounded like fun, so Mom said, "We can be
copycats and eat the same food Dad eats!"

When it was my turn to talk, I told Dad about the new girl I met on our block.

She had come over and said, "Hi, I'm Sam. My family just moved into the house on the corner. My dad is a sailor, so he's on a cruise with the Marines."

Suddenly, I didn't feel so alone. The ball of yarn in my stomach was gone!

"I'm Emily," I said, "My dad is on a cruise, too!"

Sam looked surprised.

Once our moms met, we learned that our
dads were on the same ship. Sam and I were excited.
"Wow!" she said, "Our dads can be friends, too!"
She knew all about the sailors' special food days,
but she had never heard of a paper chain. She liked
mine, so we made one for her house. Sam proudly
showed me the big jar of chocolate candy she uses to
count the days until her father comes home.

When we reached the halfway circle on our
chains, our moms had a little party for us. Sam and I ate
our candy and wore our circles like bracelets. We drew
curvy lines with our fingers on Dad's giant world map,
tracing where our fathers' ship had traveled.

After Dad had been gone a long, long time, the chain had become very short. He would be coming home soon! When there were only ten circles left, Mom and I met with other families to paint Welcome Home signs to hang at the Navy base.

Mom said, "We'll have a big party at the base when Dad and the other pilots and sailors fly home."

Finally, there was only one circle left hanging on the wall. Dad was coming home tomorrow! I saw pictures in my mind of him coming home to Mom and me.

The next morning, Mom and I hung American flags and a Welcome Home sign on the house to surprise Dad. Then we got dressed up and drove to the base.

Sam and her mom were already there.

Everyone looked up at the sky waiting to see the airplanes. When they came, I jumped up and down and waved. The planes flew close together like a capital V above our heads. I covered my ears, but I could still hear the jet engines roaring.

After the airplanes parked, the flight crews
took off their helmets and climbed down the wing
ladders.

Mom pointed and yelled, "There he is, Emily!"
We ran toward Dad. He picked me up high in
the air and then gave Mom and me a big hug.

"Dad, the chain is gone!" I shouted.
"That's right!" he said, with a big smile.
"The chain is gone, and your dad is home!"